THIS BOOK BELONGS TO

SBN 361 00458 3

Published by Purnell Books, Paulton, Bristol,
BS18 5LQ, a member of the BPCC group of companies.
Reprinted 1983
Made and printed in Great Britain by Purnell and Sons
(Book Production) Ltd, Paulton, Bristol.

NODDY
AND HIS CAR

by

Enid Blyton

CONTENTS

PICTURES BY BEEK

LONDON
SAMPSON LOW, MARSTON & CO. LTD.
AND DENNIS DOBSON LTD.

THEY GOT OUT OF THE CAR AND WENT INTO THE FAIR.
THEY LOOKED ALL AROUND

6

NODDY IS HAPPY

LITTLE Noddy woke up very happy one morning. He sat up in bed and wondered why.

"Why do I feel so glad?" he said. "Why do I want to sing and shout?"

Then he suddenly remembered. "Of course, of course! I've got a dear little red and yellow car of my very own, and I'm going to take passengers in it and be a taxi-driver!"

His little round wooden head began to nod madly. It always did when he was feeling very pleased. People were surprised when they saw his head nid-nid-nodding, but he couldn't help it. His head was fastened to his neck by a spring, you see.

"Hurrah, hurrah, I've got a fine car, it'll take me far, tra-la-la-la-LA!" sang Noddy, jumping out of bed and going to wash himself. "Dear me, how very clever I am this morning! That sounded like poetry."

"Hurray, hurray, I'm happy today, my car is so gay, hey-tiddley-hey!" sang Noddy, as he began to dress. "Dear dear me—who would believe I could make up funny little songs like that?"

He put his head out of the window and looked down into his garden. He hadn't a garage yet, so he had had to leave his car in the garden. Noddy gazed at it in delight. How lovely it looked!

8

HE HADN'T A GARAGE YET SO HE HAD TO
LEAVE HIS CAR IN THE GARDEN

"All red and yellow, and bright and shining!" said Noddy, his head nodding again. "I shall keep it so very clean. What a good thing it didn't rain in the night. It would have got very wet."

He put on his shoes and did up the laces. He put on his hat with the bell at the top. It rang loudly as he ran about, getting his breakfast.

"I must build a little garage," thought Noddy, listening for the milkman to come. He soon heard him coming along shouting "Milko! Milko!"

Noddy went to the door. "One bottle, please. And how do you like my car?"

"Simply wonderful," said the milkman. "Is that the one you got for being clever enough to find all the cars that were stolen from Mr. Golly's garage one night?"

"Yes, it is," said Noddy, nodding happily. "It was so kind of Mr. Golly to give me a car of my own. I'm going to be a taxi-driver, Mr. Milko. I want to earn some money to build a little garage."

"I'll tell everybody you're a taxi-driver then," said the milkman kindly. "How much do you charge?"

"I haven't thought yet," said Noddy, taking his bottle of milk. "Do *you* know?"

"I should say sixpence all the way there and back," said the milkman.

"Yes, I will," said Noddy. "Thank you for your help. I'll just get the money for the milk."

"No, I don't want it this morning," said Mr. Milko. "Just let me tap your head hard, Noddy, and set your head nid-nodding for ages!"

So Noddy let him, and Mr. Milko gave him such a hard tap on the head that Noddy's little wooden head nodded like mad, and the bell on his hat tinkled like a musical box.

"I hope I don't hurt you when I tap you so hard," said the milkman. "But it is such fun to see you nod so quickly."

"You don't hurt me a bit," said Noddy. "You see, my head is made of wood. Goodbye, Mr. Milko. Don't forget to tell everyone I'm a taxi-driver, and I'm waiting and waiting for passengers. And tell them I charge sixpence all the way there and back."

"Goodbye," said the milkman and off he went, shouting "Milko! Milko!" at the top of his voice. Noddy thought he was a very nice fellow indeed.

"I hope my first passenger comes soon," he thought. "Oh, I do do hope he does!"

2

NODDY'S FIRST PASSENGER

NODDY cleaned his little house, and then went to clean his beautiful car. He sang as he polished it.

> "I'm a very happy fellow,
>   I've a car of red and yellow,
>   I drive it slow or fast
>   Until we're there at last."

Mr. Tubby, the teddy bear who lived next door, put his head out of the window in surprise.

"What a nice song!" he said. "Have you had a passenger yet?"

"No," said Noddy, nodding his head. He always had to nod it, even if he wanted to shake it, because it would only nod up and down. "No. I'm waiting. I'm sure one will come. I'm just going to take my car out of the garden and put it on the road—and it will be ready."

So he took the car carefully out of the gate, and there it was, sitting in the road, waiting for its first passenger.

And will you believe it, one came! It was a pink toy cat, with a very long tail and rather fierce whiskers. She called to Noddy.

"Are you the taxi-driver? I want to go to the station, please. How much is the fare?"

"Sixpence all the way there and back," said Noddy, nodding excitedly.

" Well, I only want to go *there*, but not back," said the pink cat. "I'm going to catch the train at the station. How much is it to go there and not back?"

Noddy didn't know. He couldn't possibly do sums like that. He stared at the toy cat, puzzled.

" Well? Tell me!" said the cat, swishing her long tail. "Don't you *know*?"

Noddy nodded his head miserably. "No, I don't know," he said.

"I wish you wouldn't say *no* and nod your head at the same time," said the toy cat. "It's very muddling."

"I can't help it," said Noddy. "I'm the little nodding man. Shall we ask Mr. Tubby, the teddy bear next door, if he knows what to charge for going there and not back."

Mr. Tubby came to the door when he was called. "How much is it if we go there and not back?" asked Noddy. Mr. Tubby looked wise.

"It's exactly the same as if you go back and not there," he said, and before they could say anything more he shut the door and went inside his house.

"But can you go back if you haven't been there?" said the toy cat to Noddy, and he felt more muddled than ever. He nodded and nodded.

"Well, you know what's going to happen!" said the toy cat suddenly. "*I'm* going to miss my train! Come on—we'll decide how much to pay you when we get there."

Noddy nodded, looking cheerful again. He got into the driver's seat and took the wheel. Oh, how happy he felt to be driving his own dear little car! The toy cat got in beside him. She left her tail hanging out over the side of the car, but Noddy didn't see it. He started up the car.

17

Mr. Tubby, the teddy bear, was watching out of the window. He saw the cat's tail at once. He shouted out of the window.

"Hey, hey! Put your tail inside, toy cat!"

Noddy was so startled at Mr. Tubby's sudden shout that he put on the brake very suddenly and the toy cat shot right out of the car. Noddy nearly went, too.

The cat landed in the road. "*Now* then," she said angrily, "is *that* the way you drive a car?"

"No. Not usually," said Noddy, scared. "Oh dear. I'm so sorry. Somebody shouted and it frightened me."

" Well," said the toy cat, getting in again, "don't do *that* again. Or tell me just before you do, if you don't mind."

HE PUT ON THE BRAKE VERY SUDDENLY AND THE
TOY CAT SHOT RIGHT OUT OF THE CAR

19

Mr. Tubby shouted again, just before Noddy drove off. "HEY! You toy cat! Put your tail inside! You've left it out."

The cat put her tail inside, looking rather cross. "I don't know what business it is of that teddy bear's," she said.

Noddy drove off happily. He went down the road and everyone turned to look at him. "Parp-parp!" said his hooter proudly. "PARP-PARP!"

"Look—Noddy's got his very first passenger," said everyone, and stared after him. "There he goes. He's a proper taxi-driver now, with his very first passenger!"

3

THE TOY CAT IS VERY CROSS

THE car went over a bump and the cat's tail swung out again. Noddy saw it. "Do put it back," he said. "Really, I wish cats would look after their tails better."

"It's my tail and I can do what I like with it," said the cat, and she wouldn't put it back. And do you know, before they had gone very far it caught in the wheel of the car and came off. It did really!

The cat gave a dreadful yowl just as Noddy drove proudly into the station yard.

"My tail! I believe it's gone! Stop, stop, Noddy."

Noddy stopped. He had to, anyway, or he would have driven right on to the platform. He stared at the cat in dismay.

"What do you mean —your tail's gone?" he said. "Where's it gone?"

"How do I know, silly?" wailed the cat and jumped out of the car.

Noddy stared at her in horror. She had no tail at all now. She looked really very peculiar.

He looked round for her tail. "It must have got caught in the wheel," he said. "Oh dear—I *told* you not to leave it hanging outside the car."

There was a loud whistle and the train rushed into the station, all its carriages rumbling and clattering. It was a lovely train, a toy one, very brightly coloured.

The passengers jumped out. They were all toys except for two brownies and a little goblin.

"Quick, quick, you'll lose your train," Noddy said to the toy cat. "Never mind your tail. You can get on all right without it. *I* haven't got a tail and I manage very well."

"QUICK, QUICK, YOU'LL LOSE YOUR TRAIN,"
NODDY SAID TO THE TOY CAT

23

"Don't be so silly," wailed the cat. "Oh, you wicked little taxi-driver! I've lost my tail and now I'm going to lose my train!"

"No, no," said Noddy, pushing her to the nearest carriage. "Get in. I'll look for your tail. Oh—will you please pay me my fare-money before you go?"

"Certainly NOT!" said the toy cat. "Do you suppose *any* cat would pay a taxi-driver who chopped her tail off with the wheel of his car? *You* must pay me sixpence for a new tail!"

Before Noddy could say another word the train went off. The cat leaned over the edge of the truck and shouted at him.

"SIXPENCE! That's what you owe me. SIXPENCE! And if you don't pay me I'll tell the policeman about you. SIXPENCE!"

Noddy's head nodded unhappily. He went back to his little car and sat down in it, thinking hard. This was no way to earn money to build his dear little car a garage. Instead of earning money, he owed the toy cat sixpence for a new tail. He would have to earn that sixpence before he could earn money to buy a new garage.

He got out and looked at the wheel of his car. The tail might have got caught in it. But no—it wasn't there. It was very very sad. It was also very very stupid of the toy cat not to look after her tail better.

"I should look after my tail very well if I had one," thought Noddy. "I wouldn't leave it about like cats do. Oh dear—now I must look for another passenger."

And just then one came up. "Will you drive me to Mr. Tubby's?" he said. "I'm his brother!"

THE TEDDY BEAR'S HAT

WELL, Noddy was very pleased to have a nice teddy bear for a passenger. But Mr. Tubby's brother was fatter than Mr. Tubby, and Noddy had to push and push before he could get him into the car.

At last they were off. The car whizzed down the street, and Mr. Teddy gave a yell.

"Hey! My hat's blown off. Stop, stop!"

"Oh dear, oh dear!" thought poor Noddy. "What with tails and hats I'm not having at all a nice time."

He put on the brake, and the car slid to a stop. "You'll have to get out and find my hat," said Mr. Tubby's brother. "I'm stuck fast."

Well, Noddy couldn't *find* the hat! It had disappeared and was nowhere to be seen. The big bear was very cross about it indeed. They drove on again, Noddy nodding his head sadly. The bear grunted crossly every now and again, and looked as if he would like to bite Noddy's ear.

They got to the little house next to Noddy's at last. Noddy hooted the horn to tell Mr. Tubby that his brother had come. Then he jumped out of the car to help the big bear out.

Mr. Tubby and his plump little bear-wife came hurrying out to the gate. "Hallo, Teddy, hallo!" he cried. "Come along in."

"I'll have to get out first," said Mr. Teddy, and he heaved this way and that to free himself. But, you know, he simply couldn't get out of Noddy's car!

"Why do you have such a silly small car?" he growled at poor Noddy.

"It's you who are too fat, not my car that's too small," said Noddy, nodding his head.

"Do you *mean* to be rude?" grunted Mr. Teddy crossly. "You wait till I get out of this car."

Well, Noddy had to take the door off the car before Mr. Teddy could get out! It took him quite a long time, because he wasn't sure how to take a door off—and he was sure he would never know how to put it on again!

Mr. Teddy was out at last. Little Noddy spoke to him timidly. "Please, Mr. Teddy, sir, will you pay me my fare?"

"What nonsense is this!" growled Mr. Teddy in a very fearsome voice. "Wasn't it all because of you that I lost my fine new hat? I only bought it yesterday. You just pay me sixpence for making me lose that wonderful hat, young fellow. And stop nodding your head at me!"

Noddy could have cried. To think he wasn't going to get any money again and owed this big cross teddy bear sixpence. He remembered that he owed the toy cat sixpence, too, because she had lost her tail.

"How much are two sixpences?" he asked plump Mrs. Tubby, who was looking very sorry for him.

"They make a whole shilling," said Mrs. Tubby. "Poor Noddy. That's a lot of money. Never mind —perhaps you'll find Mr. Teddy's hat."

Noddy spent a long time putting the car door back again. He was very hungry when he had finished, but he hadn't any money to go and buy himself some dinner.

"I woke up so happy, and now I feel so sad," said Noddy to himself. "I thought it was going to be my lucky day, but it isn't. Never mind—

TO THINK HE WASN'T GOING TO GET ANY MONEY AGAIN
AND OWED THIS BIG CROSS TEDDY BEAR SIXPENCE

perhaps my next passenger will pay me a lot of money."

He got into his car when he had at last put the door on, and drove slowly down the street, looking for a passenger. He really must get a rich-looking one, who would pay him a lot of money. Then he could give the toy cat sixpence for a new tail, and could give Mr. Teddy sixpence for a new hat.

He soon saw a beautifully-dressed doll standing outside a doll's house waiting for a bus. But when she saw him she waved. " Taxi, taxi ! I want you to take me to the station, please! "

She had a little bag with her. Noddy nodded happily at her and stopped. He got out politely and opened the car door. "Get inside, Mam," he said. "We'll soon be there!"

5

POOR LITTLE NODDY

"WHAT about my bag?" said the pretty doll. "Can't you strap it on the back somewhere?"

"Oh dear," thought Noddy. "I haven't got a strap. Never mind, I'll balance it nicely on the back and watch to see that it doesn't fall off. I'll drive very slowly."

But the doll wanted to go fast. "What a beautiful little car!" she said. "But how slow. Drive fast, please, little nodding man—fast, faster, faster!"

Noddy was pleased to show how fast his car would go, and he quite forgot about the bag balanced at the back. So when he got to the station it wasn't there!

"Oooh," said Noddy, when he got out. "Your bag's gone!"

"How *careless* of you!" said the doll crossly. "And I haven't time to go back now and look for it. Here is my train coming in. You must go back and look for it and put it on the next train for me."

"Suppose I don't find it?" asked Noddy in a small voice. "I might not. Things disappear, you know."

"Then you will have to pay me sixpence," said the doll, getting out. "And I shan't pay you *any* money at all for driving me to the station, because you have been so careless."

Tears came into Noddy's bright blue eyes.

34

This was really dreadful. Whatever was he going to do? He watched the cross doll get into a carriage and then he got into his little car again.

He drove back the way he had come looking out for the bag. But he couldn't see it anywhere. It had quite disappeared.

"I'm no good as a taxi-driver," thought poor little Noddy. "No good at all. Every time I get a passenger I lose something—first a tail, then a hat, then a bag. I shall be afraid of taking any more passengers at all!"

He wondered what to do. Then suddenly he looked cheerful.

"I will go and call on dear old Big-Ears the Brownie," he thought. "He's my friend and he will help me. Yes—that's what I'll do."

So he drove off to Big-Ears' toadstool house in the woods, and when he got there he tooted loudly on the horn. Big-Ears came at once.

"Noddy! You've come to see me! I'm so glad. How are you getting on? I suppose you've made a LOT of money."

"I haven't," said Noddy, looking gloomy again. "I've had three passengers, and they haven't paid me anything—and I owe them each sixpence."

Big-Ears was most astonished. "But why? What have you been doing, Noddy?"

"Nothing, except lose things," said Noddy, and he told Big-Ears about the tail, the hat and the bag. "And I'm so hungry," he wailed. "And I'm so miserable. And I was so happy when I woke up this morning. Do you know, Big-Ears, I even sang songs I made up out of my own head?"

BIG-EARS WAS MOST ASTONISHED. "BUT WHY? WHAT HAVE YOU BEEN DOING, NODDY?"

" That's very clever of you," said Big-Ears, taking Noddy into his toadstool house. " I could never do that. Now look—here is a bit of meat-pie and a lettuce and some fresh raspberries and cream. They will make you feel better. You eat those, and I'll think what to do."

Noddy was so sad that even the sight of such a nice dinner didn't make his head nod as it should. So Big-Ears gave it a tap, and it began to nod madly.

"That's better," said Big-Ears. "That's more like you, little nodding man. I like to hear the bell jingle at the top of your hat. Now eat away—and I'll think hard."

So Noddy ate and ate—and Big-Ears thought and thought. Would he think of a good idea? Noddy *did* hope that he would!

6

BIG-EARS IS CLEVER

"I FEEL better," said Noddy at last. "Have you thought of something, Big-Ears?"

"Yes," said Big-Ears. "SOMEbody must have found all those things. We'll go back to Toyland and we'll drive slowly round the streets and watch for somebody with a new hat, or a pink tail, or a bag like the one that was lost."

"Yes," said Noddy. "We will. Let's go now. Or shall we wash-up first?"

"No. We'll go," said Big-Ears. "I'm longing to have a ride in your dear little car, Noddy. I'll be your fourth passenger and bring you luck!"

So off they went, speeding down the woodland path, scaring the rabbits dreadfully when they hooted. "Sorry to frighten you, rabbits," called Big-Ears, "but we're in a hurry. Parp-parp!"

They came back to Toyland. "Look," said Big-Ears. "There's a fair on today. Now I'm sure everybody will be there, and we may find someone with the things we're looking for."

They got out of the car and went into the fair. They looked all round—and suddenly Big-Ears tugged at Noddy's arm.

"Look—do you see that golliwog wearing that hat? It's quite new and much too big for him. It can't be his! Does it look like Mr. Teddy's?"

"Oooh yes—it does," said Noddy. "It is! But what a BAD golliwog to find someone's new hat and wear it."

"Very bad," said Big-Ears, and he marched up to the golliwog. Before the golly knew what Big-Ears was doing he had whipped the big hat off his head and was looking inside it.

"YOU JUST TELL ME IF YOUR NAME IS TEDDY TUBBY,"
SAID BIG-EARS JUST AS FIERCELY

41

"Here—what do you think you're doing with my hat!" shouted the golliwog angrily.

"You just tell me if your name is Teddy Tubby," said Big-Ears just as fiercely. "See? That's the name in this hat. Where did you get it?"

The golliwog stared at the name inside the hat and looked very frightened. He suddenly took to his heels and fled through the crowd, almost knocking three little dolls over.

"Well—we've got the hat," said Big-Ears, and Noddy nodded madly, very pleased indeed.

"You are clever, Big-Ears," he said. "Very, very clever. I do like you for my friend."

They walked through the crowds again and then Big-Ears tugged once more at Noddy's arm. He pointed to a clockwork mouse. Noddy stared.

The mouse had tied a bag on his back and was looking very important indeed. "Yes," he was saying to a little wooden horse, "I'm going on holiday. Do you see my beautiful bag? I found

it today, and as people go on holiday with
bags like this I thought I would, too. The
only thing is, I don't know how to open
the bag."

"Pray let me!" said Big-Ears, walking up to
the mouse. He untied the bag and opened it.
Inside was sewn a name: "Angela Golden-Hair".

43

"Dear *me!*" said Big-Ears. "What are *you* doing with Angela Golden-Hair's bag, I should like to know? You very naughty little mouse! Why didn't you go to the police-station and give this bag to . . ."

But the mouse was gone, squeaking in fright, running fast on his clockwork wheel. The wooden horse stared solemnly at Big-Ears and Noddy.

"He always *was* a bad little mouse," he said. " What he wants is a good spanking."

"He'll get it next time I meet him," said Big-Ears. "Well, well, Noddy, we're getting on. Now to look for the tail. Let's look hard at all the toy animals we see."

But that wasn't much good, of course, because none of them wore more than one, and Big-Ears felt certain they all belonged to them. HOW could he find the lost tail? It really was a puzzle.

EVERYTHING IS FOUND

IT was Noddy who saw the tail first! He really could hardly believe his eyes when he saw it. Nobody was wearing it as a tail—but somebody was wearing it as a fur!

Yes—there, in front of them, was little Sally Sly, who worked at the toy farm, a naughty little doll if ever there was one! She wore what looked like a very nice pink fur round her neck, and was very proud of it indeed.

Noddy pointed to it in astonishment. "It's the toy cat's tail!" he whispered. "She's wearing it round her neck like a fur. Oh, *isn't* she naughty!"

"Very," said Big-Ears. He walked up to the little doll.

"Sally Sly," he said, "why are you wearing the toy cat's tail? She wants it. Do you want her to come after you and scratch you with her sharp claws and hiss at you?"

"Oh, no, no, no!" cried the little doll, and she took the tail off at once. "How was I to know it was a tail? People shouldn't go throwing their tails away in the street like that."

"And you shouldn't take things that don't belong to you," said Big-Ears sternly. "Now where is the toy cat? We'd better find her."

46

Sally Sly fled away, crying. Dear dear—to think she had been wearing the toy cat's tail! Whatever would she say to her when next she met her?

"Well, isn't that lovely?" said Big-Ears to Noddy. "We've got everything back! Everything. Now we'll go and give them to their owners—and they must pay you the money they owe you for their fare."

So back they went to the car and got in. Big-Ears held the bag firmly on his knee and put Mr. Teddy Tubby's big hat on his head, on top of his own hat. Noddy wound the cat's tail round his neck. They weren't going to lose any of the three things again!

They went into the town and were just going round a corner when Big-Ears shouted to Noddy to stop. He stopped so suddenly that the bag shot off Big-Ear's knee into the road, and Big-Ears had to get out and get it.

"Look, Noddy!" called Big-Ears, waving his hand to some big notices on the wall. "I'll read you what these say. Listen."

Noddy listened while Big-Ears read out loud. "Reward offered to anyone finding my tail. Apply to the Toy Cat." "Reward offered to anyone finding my hat. Apply to Mr. Teddy Tubby." "Reward offered to anyone finding my bag. Apply Angela Golden-Hair."

"Good gracious!" said Noddy. "Why, we've got them all. What's a reward, Big-Ears?"

"What you get if you find something that's lost," said Big-Ears. "I expect they will pay you for each of these."

"Oooh," said Noddy, but he was very quiet when they drove off again.

"GOOD GRACIOUS!" SAID NODDY. "WHY WE'VE
GOT THEM ALL"

"What's the matter?" asked Big-Ears. "You are very quiet, and you're hardly nodding at all. I can't even hear your bell jingling on your hat."

"Well, it's like this," said Noddy. "I don't want any reward. You see, it was really through my carelessness that the bag was lost. And I was going so fast that Mr. Teddy's hat blew off. And I wasn't looking after the toy cat properly, though I *knew* she might leave her tail outside the car—so you see . . ."

"I see that you are a very nice little fellow," said Big-Ears. "Well, we'll take everything back, and at least you'll get your fare-money. I'll see to that."

They drove to the toy cat's little house. Big-Ears got out and knocked at the door. Noddy was rather afraid. Was the toy cat still very very cross?

8

NODDY IS HAPPY AGAIN

THE toy cat opened the door. She squealed
when she saw her tail. "My tail!" she cried.
"Wait—I'll give you the reward!"

"I don't want it!" called Noddy. "I should
have looked after you better. Just give Big-Ears
my fare-money, that's all."

"I shall give you two whole sixpences," said
the toy cat. "And I shall *always* use your taxi
when I want to go to the station!"

Well, wasn't that wonderful! Two whole six-pences! Noddy could hardly believe it. He drove off with Big-Ears to Angela Golden-Hair's house. She was back home again now, and when she saw her bag she almost cried for joy.

"Oh, I never thought I'd get it back!" she said. "Never! Wait, and you shall have the reward."

"I don't want it!" called Noddy happily. "It was my fault that it was lost. Just let me have my fare-money, please."

"You shall have double!" said Angela, and she gave him two sixpences. He could hardly believe his eyes. Two *more* sixpences! Well, well, well!

"And I shall always ask you to take me to the station when I need a taxi," called the pretty doll. "You're so nice and honest."

Noddy's head nodded so fast when he drove off that the bell on his hat almost played a tune. "Aren't people nice?" he said to Big-Ears.

"Well, you are too," said Big-Ears, holding on to Mr. Teddy's big hat, because Noddy was driving very fast indeed. "Be careful, Noddy. I'll be losing my whiskers if you drive too fast!"

Noddy drove slowly at once, and gazed at Big-Ears in alarm. It would be dreadful if *he* lost something, too. Big-Ears grinned back. "It's all right," he said, "they grow very tightly. I shan't really lose them."

They came to Noddy's own little house. It was next to Mr. Tubby Bear's house, where Mr. Teddy, his brother, had gone that morning. Noddy felt very brave now. He marched up to the door himself and knocked—blam, blam, blam!

Mrs. Tubby opened it. Noddy held out Mr. Teddy's big hat. "Will you give it to him?" he said. "Big-Ears and I got it back for him."

Mr. Teddy came into the hall and grunted joyfully when he saw his hat. "I offered a reward for it," he said. "You shall have it."

"WELL, I DON'T KNOW HOW MUCH IT WAS, BUT HERE
ARE TWO SIXPENCES FOR YOU," SAID MR. TEDDY

"I don't want it," said Noddy. "I drove too fast and made your hat fly off. All I want is my fare-money, Mr. Teddy."

"Well, I don't know how much it was, but here are two sixpences for you," said Mr. Teddy. "And I've been hearing such nice things about you from my brother Mr. Tubby, little Noddy, that I want to say I'm sorry for being cross. When I go home again will you please take me all the way in your nice little car? I will pay you well."

"Oh *yes*," said Noddy, beaming and nodding. "Oh, I'd *love* to, Mr. Teddy. Oh, you really *are* kind. Look, Big-Ears, two more sixpences! Aren't I lucky?"

"You deserve to be, you dear, funny little fellow," said Big-Ears. "Now come along—it's late. We've missed our tea. We'll go and buy some supper and have it in your little house, and I'll spend the night with you."

"That will be lovely!" said Noddy happily.

"And tomorrow, Noddy, tomorrow, we'll buy some lovely toy bricks with some of that money, and I'll help you to build a little garage for your car," said Big-Ears.

Noddy was too happy for words. " Come on," he said at last. "Jump into the car and we'll go and buy some supper. It's a lovely evening, Big-Ears. It won't rain tonight, I'm sure. My little car won't get wet."

Off they went together to buy their supper. Big-Ears was happy because he had put things right for his friend, and Noddy was happy because everything had come right again, and he didn't owe a lot of money after all.

Best of all he had got Big-Ears staying for supper, and sleeping with him that night. Everything was lovely.

"I feel just as happy now as I felt this morning when I woke up," said Noddy suddenly, and he began to sing, his bell jingling like music.

"I've got a house
   And a car of my own,
   I've got a friend
   So I'm never alone,
   I feel so happy
   I'm singing a song,
   And if I'm not careful
   I'll sing all night long!"

"Oh no you won't," said Big-Ears, squeezing Noddy's arm. "I shall want some sleep. How *clever* you are, Noddy, singing songs out of your own head. I never, never knew you were as clever as that."

"Nor did I," said Noddy. "Oh, Big-Ears, it's fun being me. I like it. Do you suppose I'll have lots more adventures some day?"

"Yes," said Big-Ears, "you will. I'm sure of it."

I'm sure, too. I'll tell you the next one as soon as it happens!

LOOK FOR
THE
NEXT
NODDY
BOOK

BEEK